Squeaky Clean

For Miranda and Euan, with love – SP
For Chris P. with Love – MM

SQUEAKY CLEAN
A RED FOX BOOK 0 09 941349 3

First published in Great Britain by The Bodley Head,
an imprint of Random House Children's Books

The Bodley Head edition published 2001
Red Fox edition published 2003

1 3 5 7 9 10 8 6 4 2

Text copyright © Simon Puttock, 2001
Illustrations copyright © Mary McQuillan, 2001

The right of Simon Puttock and Mary McQuillan to be identified as the author and illustrator of this
work has been asserted in accordance with the Copyright, Designs and Patents Act 1988

Red Fox Books are published by Random House Children's Books,
61–63 Uxbridge Road, London W5 5SA,
a division of The Random House Group Ltd,
in Australia by Random House Australia (Pty) Ltd,
20 Alfred Street, Milsons Point, Sydney, NSW 2061, Australia,
in New Zealand by Random House New Zealand Ltd,
18 Poland Road, Glenfield, Auckland 10, New Zealand,
and in South Africa by Random House (Pty) Ltd,
Endulini, 5A Jubilee Road, Parktown 2193, South Africa

THE RANDOM HOUSE GROUP Limited Reg. No. 954009
www.kidsatrandomhouse.co.uk

A CIP catalogue record for this book is available from the British Library.

Printed in Singapore

Squeaky Clean

Simon Puttock & Mary McQuillan

RED FOX

Mama Pig had three little piglets, and when they were new, they were all clean and beautiful. But, being piglets, they soon got grubby.

"Oh, you mucky piglets," said Mama Pig. "Tonight, you shall all have a bath."

"No, no, NO!" squealed the three little piglets. "We do not WANT to be clean!"

"Yes, yes, YES!" said Mama Pig firmly. "You are three little sillies, and you shall be scrubbed."

And she scooped them all up and popped them into the tub. But...

"It's too deep," squealed Piglet One.
"It's too WET!" squealed Piglet Two.
"Eek, EEK, EEK!" squealed Piglet Three.

And they squirmed and they wormed and they would NOT be washed.

"I think," said Mama Pig, "that this bath needs some...

...bubbles!" And she swished and
she swashed and she made lots of froth.

"Oooh, bubbles are pretty," said Piglet One.
"Bubbles are tickly," said Piglet Two.
"Hee, hee, hee!" said Piglet Three.
"Now," said Mama Pig, "it's time for...

...ducks." And plop, plop, plop, three rubber ducks dropped into the tub.

plop

plop

plop

"I like ducks," said Piglet One.

"Ducks are fun," said Piglet Two.
"Quack, quack, quack!" said Piglet Three.

"And NOW," said Mama Pig, "for...

...splishy splashy sploshy." And she splooshed and she swooshed and galooshed them all over.

"More, more, more!" said Piglet One.
"Please sploosh ME!" said Piglet Two.
"Wheeeeeeee!" said Piglet Three. And he wriggled and he giggled and he piggled with glee.
It was a very best bathtime.

Mama Pig dried them and kissed them and patted
their heads.

"Time for bed, my piglets," she said, and she
popped them in between the sheets.

"And NOW," said Mama Pig to herself,
"it is MY bathtime."

Mama Pig had LOTS
of bubbles, and rubber
ducks, and
a lovely,
long wallow.

Then she towelled,

and powdered,

and when she was done,
she opened the door,
and there she saw...

...her three little piglets, all clean and beautiful,
sneak, sneak, sneaking down the hall.

"Just where do you think you're going?" asked Mama Pig.

"We are going to get GRUBBY again!" they said.

"Oh, you BAD, NAUGHTY piglets," said Mama Pig,
"I've just this minute got you beautiful and clean."

"Indeed," agreed the piglets three. "We are all clean and beautiful, and very nice it is too. But we want you to give us another bath, because baths are the BEST FUN!"

Mama Pig laughed and laughed.

"Oh, you GOOD little piglets, you SHALL have another bath, but two in one day are just too much. You shall all have another tomorrow."

And she scooted them back to bed.

"Goodnight, piglets," said Mama Pig.

"Goodnight, Mama,"
said Piglet One.

"Goodnight, Mama,"
said Piglet Two.

But there wasn't a peep from Piglet Three,
because Piglet Three was...

Hee! Hee! Hee!
...splish splash sploshing all over again!

OTHER TITLES YOU MIGHT ENJOY

WHO'S POORLY TOO?
Kes Gray and Mary McQuillan

SHADOWHOG
Sandra Ann Horn and Mary McQuillan

OUR TWITCHY
Kes Gray and Mary McQuillan

EAT YOUR PEAS
Kes Gray and Nick Sharratt

TINY
Paul Rogers and Korky Paul

FRIENDS TOGETHER
Rob Lewis

KATIE MORAG'S ISLAND STORIES
Mairi Hedderwick

HOLD TIGHT!
John Prater

BABY KNOWS BEST
Kathy Henderson and Brita Granstrom

NAUGHTY!
Caroline Castle and Sam Childs